ISBN: 978-93-55463-18-0
eISBN: 978-93-55463-19-7

© Publishers

Publisher: Pharos Books (P) Ltd.
Plot No.-55, Main Mother Dairy Road
Pandav Nagar, East Delhi-110092 (India)
Phone: +014049995474
WhatsApp: +014049995474
E-mail: sales@pharosbooks.in
Website: www.pharosbooks.in
Edition: 2021

AESOP'S SECRET BOOK#1
Author: Cristina Kay

Cristina Kay

Ages: 6+

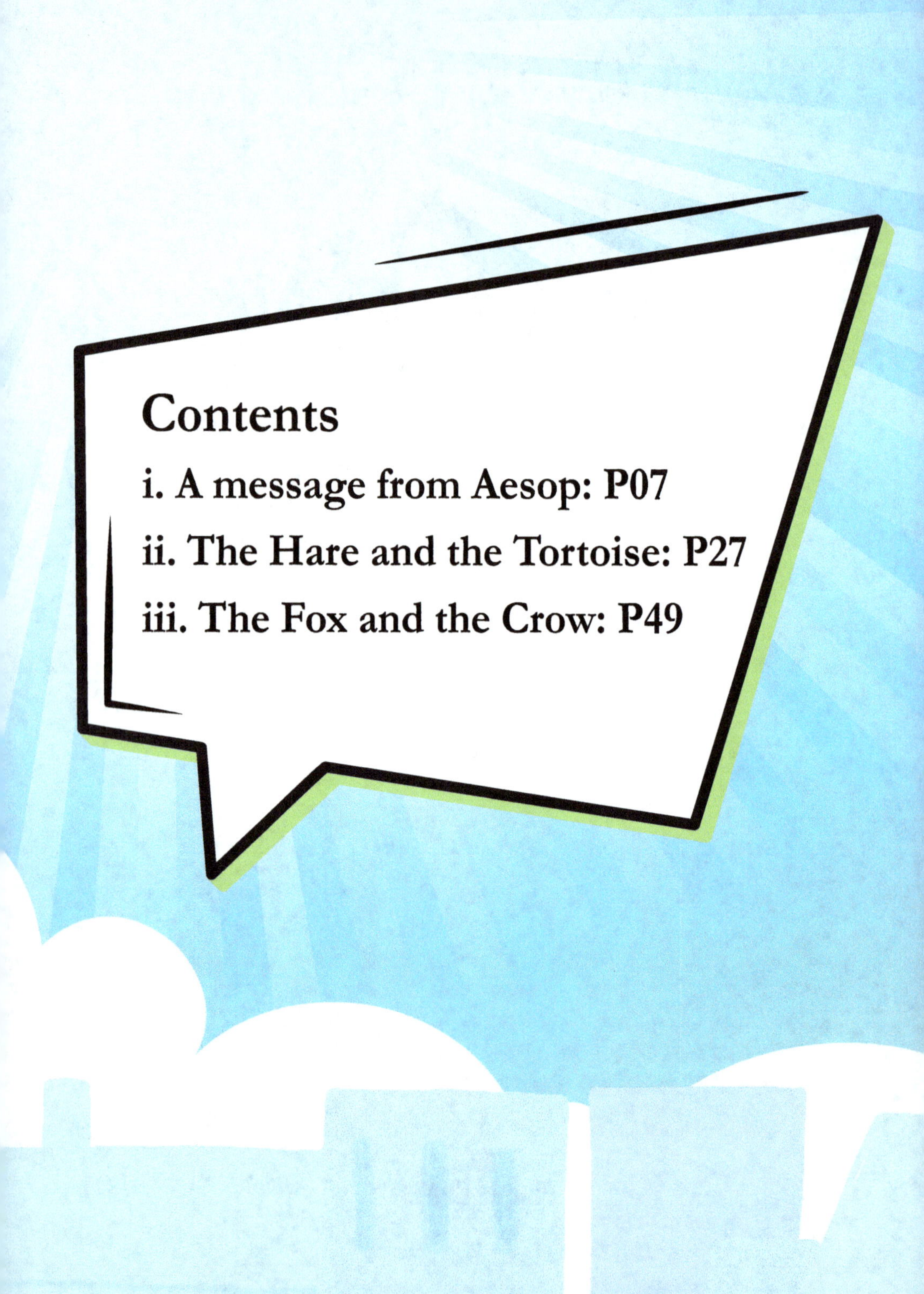

Contents

" To all the children on Earth who dream
of a better world."

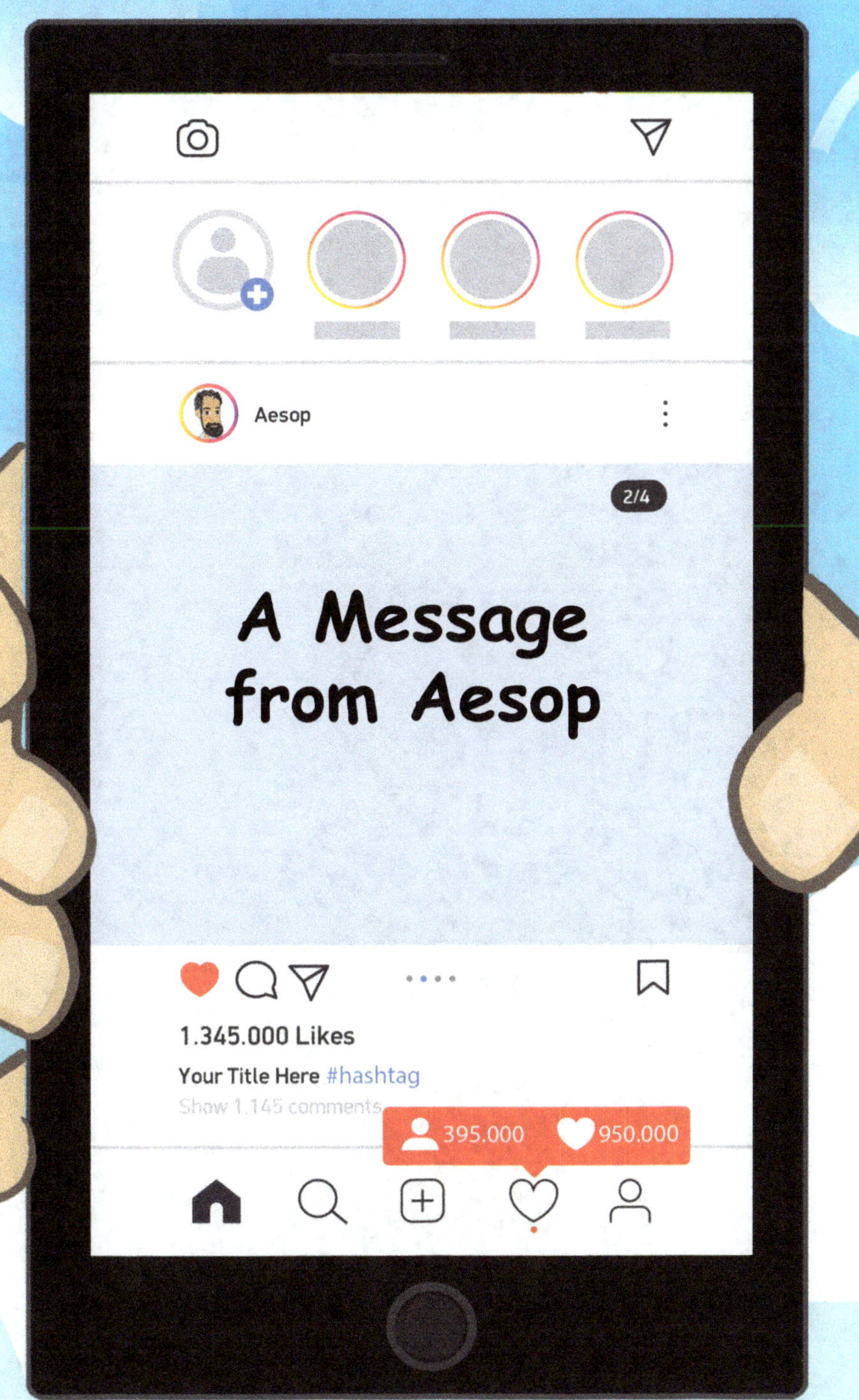

Aesop
2/4
A Message
from Aesop
1.345.000 Likes
Your Title Here #hashtag
Show 1.145 comments
395.000
950.000

Hey, kids!
I'm Aesop!
I'm sure you've heard I'm the wisest storyteller in the world, according to all great men and those who have read my fables.
I lived many centuries ago, yet my reputation lives to date.

Back in my time, the world was different. People didn't know how to read or write, that's why they thought in a different way. Whatever happened, even knowledge, travelled by word of mouth. That's the case with my fables as well. As so many people liked them, they narrated them to one another for a long time, for hundreds of years - yeah, you read that correctly -, so they weren't forgotten.

Then, writing was invented and people made my stories into a book.
I was really touched, although I had long departed from this world, since my mission had come to an end.
I was on the planet of the Wise Storytellers. "Is there such a planet?" you may ask. Sure there is! If you ask me what it's like, I won't tell you any details as I'd love to know how you imagine it. That would be interesting, right?

So, I ended up on this planet, my only companion Ancient the Owl. I won't say much about her either. It's better for you to get to know her through the stories you are going to read, for I'm sure you're going to be thrilled.

All I have to say is that she was the owl of Greek Goddess Athena and we never parted, even when I left Earth. We were and still are inseparable.

At first, no one else but me lived on the planet of the Wise Storytellers. My days were joyful, though, as I shared them with the heroes of my fables, who were none other than animals. While I was still on Earth, I liked observing animals' behaviours and found out that they were much like those of humans.

Using animals, these precious creatures, as examples, I sent messages to humans through my stories. I told them what to do in order to become better and happier. It was these precious beings that gave messages to humans through my stories. Of course, those were different times and different messages.

With the passage
of time, my company
grew with more Wise
Storytellers that keep
coming here,
so I'm becoming happier
and happier.

Of course, I must tell you that one of my
favourite pastimes all these centuries has been
to go down on Earth once in a while. You see, I've
always been curious and interested in observing
developments by myself. What was happening with
humans, especially children. So much had stayed the
same and so much more had changed since my time.
On the one hand, I saw there were still
fracas, rows and wars, just like in my
era, but on the other so many important
things took place. Important new
things that I wanted to study.

So, sometimes I would come back in the form of a Library fairy that stayed up at night, reading new books. I was so enthusiastic that I occasionally left the oil lamp on, while there was no electricity on Earth.

   Hearing the librarian wonder how this could be possible, since he checked everything before he locked the door, I hid under the reading tables, so that he wouldn't find me; I didn't want to get into trouble.

Other times, I became the tom cat of a bookshop that curled up at the display window.

I remember purring with satisfaction as I saw humans greet one another, taking off their tall hats, then searching for books with new ideas and talking for hours on end.
Each time, I'm impressed by so many changes!

BOOKSHOP

Over the past years, I've been transforming into a dove. I alight at the open window of a classroom, enjoying the lesson and the children's wonderful discussions on how the world can become even better. Then, they share all this with far-flung children, inside magic boxes, called computers.

When this happened, you can't imagine how thrilled I was! I found out I could make up my own stories in an ebook and email them to all the kids! Not to mention that they can print out whichever they like! That's amazing, isn't it? You may ask me where I found the computer. Well, could the planet of the Wise Storytellers not keep pace with technology or go without computers? Think about it…

The time I've been dreaming of for centuries has finally come! I can't hide my joy!

You'll ask me what these secret stories are.

It's a book I took with me when I came from the planet of the Wise Storytellers and guarded it while I was on Earth. Back then, I didn't tell anyone that I knew how to write when everyone else didn't. It was too soon to say such a thing, no matter how strange this may sound to you. It was also too soon, centuries ago, for me to narrate the stories I had written for the future.

The roughest patch I had to go through, when my book was in real danger, was when I was threatened by the planet of the Angry Brawlers, quite a few years ago. One day, all of a sudden, they sent me a horrendous message dangling from a comet's tail:

"For Aesop, leader of the Wise Storytellers.

Give us your secret book or we are going to destroy your planet."

That was the only time in my life that I got really scared. Where had they learnt about that? On the planet I come from, nobody gives away secrets. Some people say that they have a magic ball where they can see everything, but I can't tell this with certainty.

Still, I was sure that, if the book fell into their hands, they would wipe it off forever.

If this happened, it would be a disaster as it would serve their dark plans. In a few words, the Angry Brawlers, young and old, wanted to be at loggerheads all the time. And they did all they could to make it.

I decided to speak to the Wise Storytellers and the animals on my planet. I summoned leaders from the nearby galaxies. Everyone agreed in unison that the Angry Brawlers had to learn a good lesson and let people be, so that they could live a better life. As the secret book would help them on this score, it had to be saved at all costs.

Now I'm sure you're expecting to read what triggered a tough war that lasted for days, even months.

Still, no war broke out!

That's impossible, you'll say. Still, it is, as you'll see later on.

When the Angry Brawlers approached us on board
their formidable spaceships, they were in for a
surprise. Upon seeing that we had an entire army
of planets by our side, while they were alone, they
didn't know what to do. They couldn't believe
their eyes.

So, they turned on
their heels and beat a
nasty retreat. It was such
a funny spectacle!
Standing united
and fearless, we managed,
not only to turn them away,
but also to force them to
go to a remote planet, far
away from their own.

There, even if they have the magic ball,
they can't see anything because of the distance.
So, you can understand that they're completely
harmless.

Our feast after the victory can't be put into words. I can tell you only one thing: It's still going on as I write these lines.

So, my beloved children, my secret book was saved and it's time to pop up on screen or on your library shelf.

Here, you will enjoy the first two stories a little different from what you already know it, but I'm

sure you'll find it so interesting that you will hold lots of conversations about it with your friends, parents and teachers.

I bid you farewell with a promise to see you again soon.

Aesop

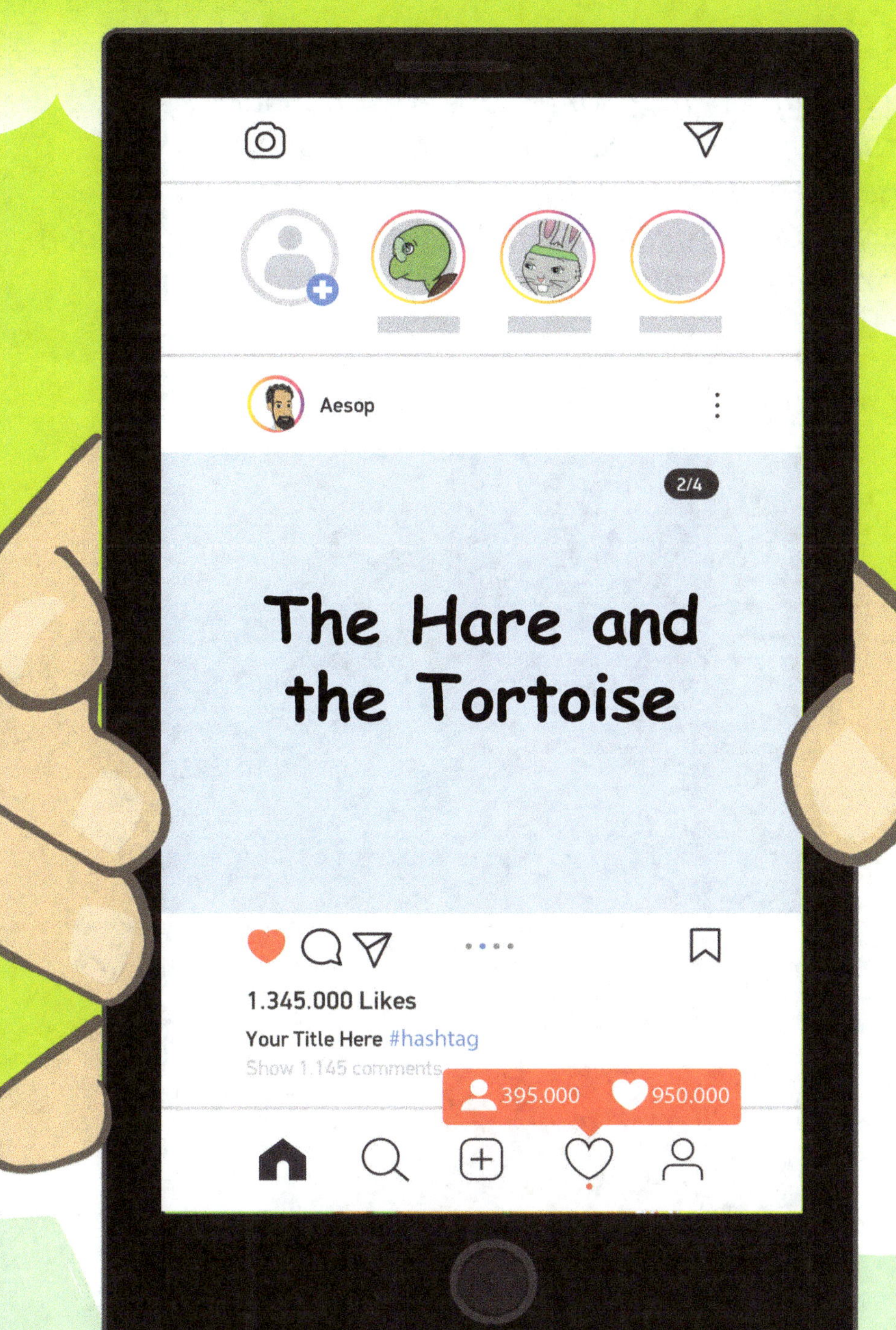

Aesop
2/4
The Hare and
the Tortoise
1.345.000 Likes
Your Title Here #hashtag
Show 1.145 comments
395.000
950.000

When the spring sun rays came out of the thick tree foliage, they found Speedy the Hare seated outside his nest chewing a tender carrot.

He spent his days eating carrots, training and taunting the forest animals, since they couldn't run as fast as he could.

He always came up with something insulting. When he wanted to have some fun, he flaunted his prowess in running fast. Other hares didn't agree with his stance, but he wouldn't listen to anyone.

He was usually provocative, but today he was being bored.

Only a fancy butterfly impressively flying over the colourful blooming wildflowers caught his eye. "Fast as I am, if I also had wings, no one would beat me. I'd be even more perfect. Unique! Everyone would kneel before me," he murmured and angrily took a bite out of his carrot. The more he thought about it, the angrier he got. He had to take it out on someone.

So, when he saw Terra the Tortoise slowly going in circles around a tussock of cool grass, he burst into laughter. "You set off at dawn and cover a metre within a day," he shouted to her and cracked up.

Terra said nothing, while he continued, undaunted. "What's that chest you're carrying on your back, poor thing? It's the bane of your existence, a curse! How can you stand it?" "It's a blessing," the tortoise told him calmly and carried on with her food.

"Hehe! You're so much fun! A blessing?! I can't see any blessing!"

"My shell is knowledge and protection. I've owed my life to it for many years."

Speedy grew jealous upon hearing Terra's words.

"Can't you see how ugly you are with these funny glasses or how handsome I am? Maybe you're blind as well. Look at my body and how these shorts suit me!"
Terra was hurt by his words, so she decided not to return his insults. She had learnt that this leads nowhere and she didn't mean to get upset.
"Everyone has their gifts," she said, enjoying the taste of fresh grass.
"Where did you learn all these wisecracks? Don't tell me you thought of them with this silly head!"
"At Ancient the Owl's School."

Seething with rage, Speedy decided to humiliate her. He couldn't wrap his head around the fact that he had no wings to make them all bite the dust and a tortoise pretended to be so educated.

"Since you're a know-it-all, do you want to race each other to the river? What d' you think? Will your intelligence help you walk faster? 'Cause running is out of the question!"

Although she thought that it
was a long distance, Terra decided to give it a try.
"I'll give it a try."
The hare couldn't believe his ears.

"What a cheek!" he muttered under his breath. "Since she's asking for it, why miss the opportunity?"

"Hehe! That was the last thing I expected to hear from you. So, you do want to make a laughingstock of yourself, eh?"

The tortoise didn't speak and he continued in a disdainful way:

"Come on! Get going and I'll catch up with you!"

Terra set out at a slow but steady pace. She had covered several metres when she reached a crossroads. She stooped short and continued after a while. Speedy heaved a sigh of relief.

"She's fun. She wants to show off — poor thing!
If she were really smart, she wouldn't dare race me.
Let's enjoy the whole thing, then. I'll let her walk to
the clearing halfway through, then I'll sprint to the
finish line like the wind.
I'm going to wait for her there and, when she
arrives, she'll realise how foolish she is!"
he said to himself and swelled up
with pride.

The colourful butterfly went closer again
and began fluttering her wings, making some
impressive circles over them. Speedy was
engrossed in the spectacle and his jealousy
flared up again. He remembered that he
couldn't fly, which would make him even
more perfect. Without realising it, he got
lost in those thoughts until he was struck to
see that the sun was high in the sky.
It was noon.

He estimated the time, then stretched wearily. Making no haste, he walked into the path the tortoise had taken to get to the river. "I'm going to laugh my heart out," he said to a squirrel that happened to be passing by and gave him a puzzled look. Then, the hare started searching for the tortoise. Terra was nowhere to be found. He let his gaze wander as far away as he could. To no avail. He didn't like that at all.

He started running without even breathing.
Just before he got to the river, he saw
the tortoise from a distance on top of a rock
drinking water out of the riverbed.
She was enjoying the crystal clear water that was
running, as joyful as Terra's mood.

The hare couldn't believe his eyes. Terra the Tortoise — yes, the tortoise! — had made it to the finish line before him. How could that be? He became very angry at first, but then his anger turned to rage, then to shame within seconds. How would he appear in the forest again? All the animals would make fun of him.

It was their chance to get their own back for what he had done to them.

Without much thought, he decided to hide inside the thick foliage and never come out again. Sad as he was, he was trying to find a bush when he saw Terra approaching him, smiling from ear to ear. Then, Speedy felt even more ashamed. He remembered how he had insulted her, but she didn't even hold him a grudge or think of taking revenge, now that she was the winner. Or was he wrong?

As soon as the tortoise went up to him, he couldn't but ask her with his head bowed:

"How did you make it?"

His voice was barely audible.

"As I walk very slowly, I've learnt every single path in the forest, even the smallest and narrowest trail. So, once I reached the crossroads, I plodded on from a spot with a clump of bushes that takes a shortcut to the river. Very few know it."

"I suppose those who are just as fast as I am will never know this. I'm careless, fast and selfish, that's what I am. No one will ever want me!" said the hare and burst out crying.

The tortoise thought that the only thing that could help him would be for her to suggest a way he could turn his speed to good account.

"Let's combine my knowledge with your swiftness? What do you say? I think both are needed. Maybe we'll achieve great things if we join forces."

"You think we'll make it?" asked Speedy in surprise. He couldn't believe his ears.

"Sure we will if we want to. We have nothing to lose." From that day onwards, the two of them became inseparable and did great things.

Let's say that the tortoise made plans as to how the weakest animals would be kept out of harm's way; how they would have food during a drought; and how they would build their nests from scratch when they were blown by the wind.
As for the hare, he fixed them all in no time.

They always made sure to do something useful. The tortoise had learnt at the Great Owl's School that what was good for others was good for her as well. The hare learnt about that every day and became better and better. His swiftness had acquired a meaning now, just like the tortoise's knowledge.

Whenever they disagreed, instead of fighting, the hare went for a jog to let off steam, while the tortoise slid into her shell to think.

Upon seeing how well they worked together and how happy the two of them were, some animals decided to follow their example. So, life in the forest gradually improved for everyone.

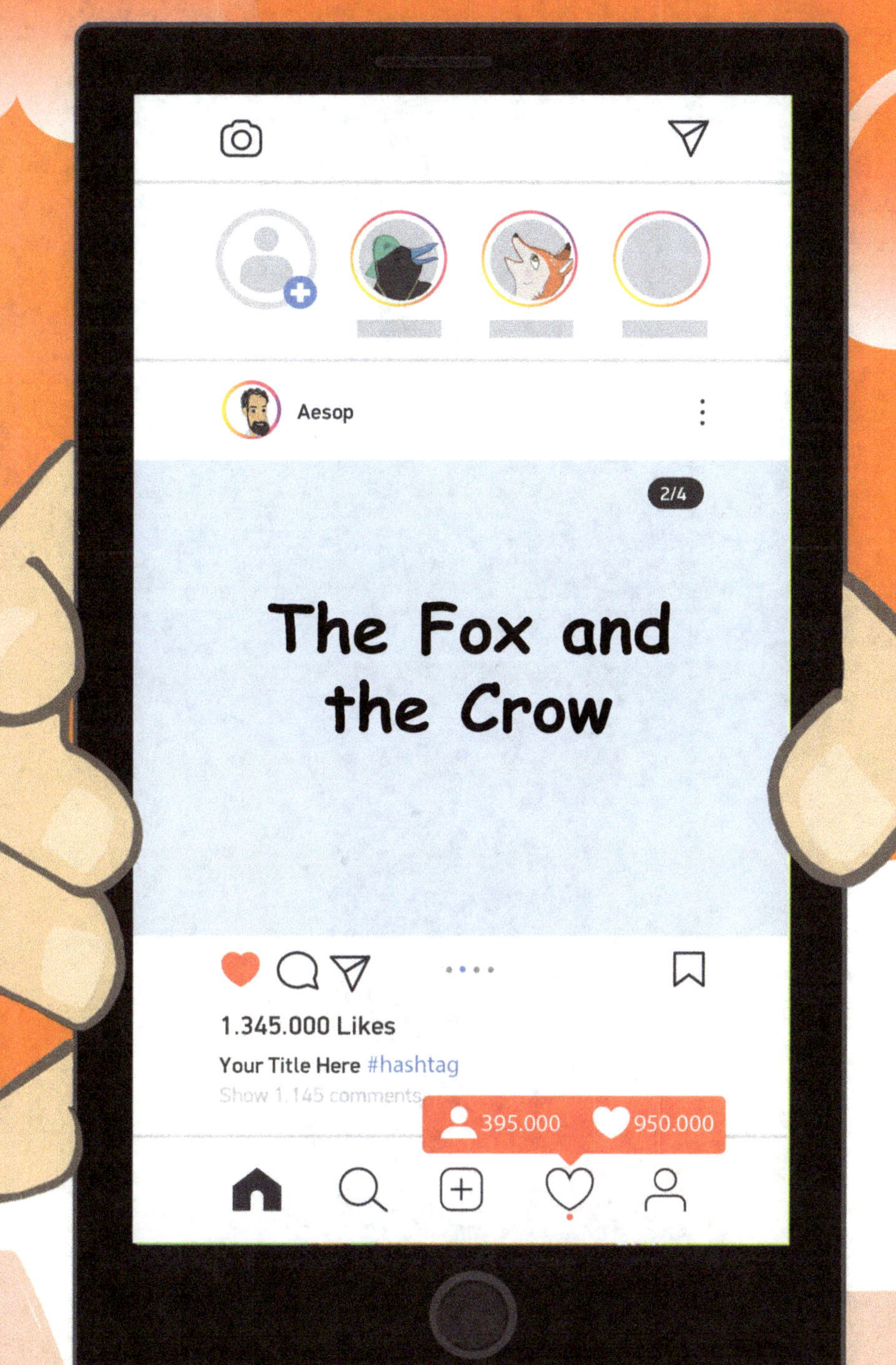

Aesop
2/4
The Fox and
the Crow
1.345.000 Likes
Your Title Here #hashtag
Show 1.145 comments
395.000
950.000

The Fox, Fiona, lay under a bushy plane tree.
She enjoyed its cool shade so much! The mountain
was magical at that time of year. Summer colours
made it look like heaven.

"Life is so beautiful when you're lazy. It's so
gruelling looking for food. It's great to have it all
done for you," she thought and didn't care one bit
about the beauty of nature in the summer.

After a while, though, her stomach began growling.

"I'm so hungry…but I'm too bored to search for
food. I should find someone I can fool to fill my
stomach."

Proud of her idea, she slyly blinked and coyly
scratched her back against the
plane tree trunk.

CAW

And she scratched and scratched until she heard a swoosh.

A crow fluttered its wings over her, holding a piece of cheese in its beak. It was so buttery that she couldn't resist it. Not to mention that it was a really big chunk! It was exactly what she needed to quell her hunger.

"Hey! I never expected to find you here! Today's my lucky day! I'll treat myself to a delicacy!" Fiona the Fox said to herself, drooling over the cheese. She then wiped her wet lips on her gaily-coloured scarf.

The crow alighted on the densest branch of the plane tree and looked at the fox without greeting her.

"You're so handsome!" Fiona buttered him up, her eyes fixed on the cheese. "You look like a lord in your black suit!" she kept praising the crow, although the only thing he wore was a cap and a golden chain with his name. "Now that I've taken a closer look at you, I can say it! Your beak is your most charming characteristic! It's so strong, the likes of which I've never seen before!"

The crow was so happy as never before had he heard such kind words and that he was good-looking. The other animals usually avoided him because of his black colour and his ugly voice, as they said. That's why he lived with other crows on the tallest slopes and spots of the mountain and learnt how to nick whatever he came across in order to eat. He always feared he would go without food.

"Come on! Don't stay silent. At least tell me your name, so that I can hear your wonderful voice," Fiona said in a mellifluous tone.

"At last, there's someone who recognizes my merit and understands not only my rare beauty, but also the magic of my voice. I never understood those who say it's discordant and scary. At last, I'll have a friend other than the other crows, an admirer!"

Many a time, the crow tried to befriend other animals as well. He wanted to participate in the forest festivities, rejoice and have fun with them. Still, all he knew was how to be a predator, which made things worse. But now he was being given a first-rate opportunity to have a new friend and he wouldn't pass it up. So, he decided to show the fox that she was right about admiring him.

"My name's Caw! I'm glad you saw how unique I am! You're so clever and deserve to be my friend!" he began to say, swelling up with pride, and went on to describe his gifts.
What great quality his plumage was, how invincible his beak.

CRA

"As for my voice, you're right. Everyone's pleasantly surprised when I open my mouth to speak."

The truth is, Caw was born with a nice voice and sang the right way, yet the other animals hadn't stopped to listen to him and they believed he was no different from the other crows.

The crow rambled on and on, looking up, so he didn't notice that the fox was smacking her lips. She had already eaten the cheese.

"You're not only a predator, but a fool and a bighead as well!" she interrupted him when she had had enough of him.

"And you are so sneaky!" the crow replied angrily when he realised he had been fooled.

"You made me sneaky! I have trouble finding food because you and your fellow crows wipe everything out in no time! Like everything's yours!"

"You and your friends are to blame became you keep us at arm's length and always make fun of our black colour!"

All hell broke loose. They blamed each other for their behaviour. They were both so angry. The crow threshed about so agitatedly on the branch that he almost lost half its feathers. As for the fox, she wagged her tail so fast as she circled the tree trunk that she almost cut it off. They were unable to communicate.

On top of that, an angry murder of crows suddenly arrayed next to Caw. They had come to his rescue. The whole sky turned black. Around Fiona, apart from the other foxes, had gathered most of the small animals of the mountain to support her.

Everyone looked ready to fight to the bitter end.
"We call the shots! Deal with it! We can wipe you out if we want!" the crows cawed.

Upon hearing that, the other animals froze in their tracks for a few seconds, but they wouldn't relent. Suddenly, a kettle of hawks were ready to attack the crows, who started shaking with fear. Never before had there been such a commotion around the area.

Everyone had got a hoarse voice when the sun marked the end of the day by taking a spectacular dip behind the mountain. Just before the moon welcomed the night, a hollow voice was heard. It came from the top of the tallest fir tree, but it was so calmly strong that it deadened all the others.

CAW

"Stop at once! If you carry on like that, a war will soon break out in the mountain. Can you imagine how bad this will be? We're all necessary. White, black, yellow, big and small. No one can exist without the other. When will you realise that?"

Once the Ancient Owl's voice was heard, a venerable silence fell all around. Her words, every time she spoke, got the animals and birds thinking. Even the most unruly ones. How would they stop fighting and fooling one another? What was it that they still hadn't understood? Laden with these thoughts, and keeping silent, they all left for their nests.

Tonight, all the inhabitants of the forest had a quiet sleep. Some of them dreamt that, as of the following day, they would try to live peacefully without disturbing one another, while others began to make their dream come true the moment they woke up as they realised they would live better only this way.

zzZZ
zzZZ

TO BE
CONTINUED

AUTHOR'S BIO

Cristina Kay (Cristina Kollias) was born in Greece. Under the affectionate sun of her country, she learnt how to care for people and be inspired by its poets and myths.

She is a writer, a social therapist and a Personal Development Counsellor. This long journey led her to research and the creation of the therapeutical method "I write-I express myself-I am released," which she presented at the Second International Conference for Creative Writing.

She is the coordinator of various Creative and Therapeutical Writing workshops and has collaborated with important agents and bodies in her country, such as the University of Athens structures.

She loves children, that is why she often shares her stories with them, either through her books, at Museums and through art, or through Nature, inspiring them to write fairytales and poems.

She does the same with adult groups as she believes that the therapeutical power of writing can reveal the wonderful child they hide deep within, so that she may help them rewrite their stories, correcting all that is necessary in order for them to live better.

She is member of the educational team of the Greek Network for Group Analysts and the Group Analytic Society International.

Six individual works, children books and poetry books, have been published in the Greek language and she has taken part in many collective works.

Some works of hers have been awarded, presented at scientific seminars and conferences and put on stage for social causes.

She lives in Athens and in her spare time she likes walking around the Acropolis or Sounion, making birthday cakes for her beloved persons and communicating with friends from all over the world.

Contact: fairytale.st@gmail.com